NORA MAEVE AND SEBI

words by Andrew Greeley
pictures by Diane Dawson

Paulist Press · New York, N.Y. · Ramsey, N.J. · Toronto, Canada

Published by: Paulist Press

Editorial Office 1865 Broadway
                  New York, New York 10023

Business Office: 545 Island Road
                 Ramsey, New Jersey 07446

Library of Congress Catalogue Card Number: 76·18047
ISBN: cloth 0.8091.0214.5 Paper 0.8091·1974·9

Printed and bound in the United States of America

Once upon a time, long, long ago (well, actually, it was last week), there lived a little girl named Nora Maeve. She had blond hair and blue eyes and was three years old.

She had a brother named Liam who also had
blond hair and blue eyes and was almost six years
old. Liam was a boy, but he was not bad as boys go.
She had a mother named Mommy who had red
hair and who wrote funny things on paper. She
had a father named Daddy who drove a silly
foreign car.
Daddy worked with a funny man named Anty who
took lots of pictures of Nora Maeve and Liam and
had a great big boat with a big blue sail. The
boat's name was Brigid.
What's a Brigid?
It's a saint, *silly!*

FUNNY
THING!

FUNNY
THINGS

FUNNY
THINGS

OUI 200

Nora Maeve was not yet quite ready to ride on
Anty's boat. The lake was too big.

Mommy and Daddy and Liam and Nora Maeve
lived in an old house on a curved street with lots
of trees on the top of the hill. The street didn't have
a name but a number.
A number is a strange name for a street.
At the foot of the hill was a Big Street called "da
Drive." Lots of teenagers drove down da Drive in
fast cars. Mommy and Daddy told Nora Maeve and
Liam to stay off da Drive because teenagers were
dangerous drivers.
Anty said that Mommy and Daddy were teenagers
once, but he must have been joking.
Mommy and Daddy were grups.
What's a grup?
A grup is a grown-up, *silly!*

Nora Maeve liked teenage girls. They brought her candy, and picked her up in their arms, and laughed with her. She didn't like teenage boys because they were so rough. But Liam liked teenage boys a lot.
Brothers are that way.
Nora Maeve liked to watch Sesame Street on television. She liked Big Bird and Ernie and Mr. Snuffagopolous. But most of all, she liked Cookie Monster.
Nora Maeve adored Cookie Monster. In fact, she adored all monsters.

Come to think of it, she adored cookies too.

She had all kinds of friends on her block. Their names were Catherine Mary, Jenny, Abbie and Libby. And there was another little girl named Nora too. That confused everybody.
And there were lots of wonderful animals on the block. There was a bird named Bingo in her own house (he wasn't much like Big Bird though). The other Nora had a big St. Bernard named 'Nelope who let both Noras ride on her back. The other Nora also had a little Schnauzer named Muffie who barked all the time. There were two dogs named Heather and Jillie who spent a lot of time at Nora Maeve's house even though they didn't live there. Come to think of it, they adored Nora Maeve. All dogs did.

But the funniest dog on the block was named...

Sebastian!

He lived across the street from Nora Maeve with his family (they had *lots* of kids) and another dog named Duncan.

Duncan was a little woolly dog. And no one ever called him anything except Duncan.

Sebastian was a great big black Labrador Retriever and everyone always called him Sebi.

What's a Sebi?

It's short for Sebastian, *silly!*

Sebi was handsome and friendly and lapped up affection like a pitcher of warm milk. He loved everyone and he wanted everyone to love him.

But he was awfully clumsy. He may just have been the clumsiest big dog in all the world.

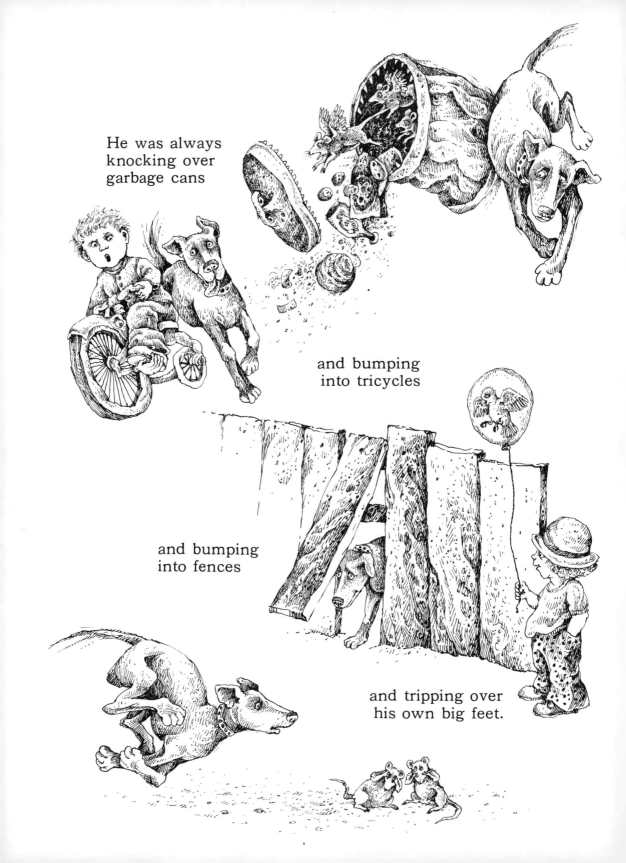

He was always
knocking over
garbage cans

and bumping
into tricycles

and bumping
into fences

and tripping over
his own big feet.

Mommy said that Sebastian (she always called him
that) was probably the dumbest dog in all the
world. But she liked him anyhow.
Sebi adored Nora Maeve.
He went crazy every time he saw her. She petted
his long funny nose and pulled his long funny ears
and hugged his long funny back. And Sebi just
ate it all up.

But one day something terrible happened.

Nora Maeve came out of the house to play with Katie. She walked down the stairs and into her driveway.

Sebi was snoozing on the front porch across the street. He sniffed the air and then opened his big dumb eyes. He picked up his long funny ear.

"Nora Maeve," said Sebi to himself and bounded across the street (he was too dumb even to look for the traffic). He ran right into the driveway and jumped up on Nora Maeve.

And he knocked her down and she tore a hole in the knee of her brand new slacks. Nora Maeve cried, and cried, and cried.

She got mad at Sebi.

"Buzz off, Sebi," she said and went crying into the house to find Mommy.

Sebi was very sad. His feelings were hurt. His big funny ears dropped. His long tail drooped. His great sad eyes looked even sadder. He went back across the street very slowly.

Nora Maeve didn't love him anymore.

Mommy was not exactly pleased. "You should stay away from that big stupid mutt," she said. "I told him to buzz off," said Nora Maeve.

But Sebi didn't really buzz off. He kept chasing
Nora Maeve.

With unperturbed pace.

The next day Nora Maeve went to school.
Her school was a real neat place. It was an old
white castle on the hill above da Drive. Nora
Maeve and the other three-year-olds made things
and colored pictures and had lots of fun. Her
pictures were almost as good as Liam's—that's
what Liam said anyway.
She looked out the window of the castle and guess
who was there with his great big funny tongue
hanging out?

You're right: it was Sebi.

"Buzz off, Sebi," said Nora Maeve.
But he didn't.
He followed her home from school tripping over
his big feet all the way.

That afternoon he hid
behind the garbage can
and waited for Nora
Maeve to come out.

Then he hid behind
the great big tree
on the front lawn.

Then he hid under
Daddy's funny foreign car.

Then he hid on the front steps.

Everywhere Nora Maeve went, there was Sebi—
his big funny mouth open and his big sad eyes
looking even sadder than usual.
"Buzz off, Sebi," said Nora Maeve.
But he wouldn't.

Liam came home from school and Sebi trotted over
to him. Maybe he would become an ally. Liam
petted Sebi but he knew what little sisters could
be like when their feelings were hurt.
"Forget it," he told Sebi.

That evening Mommy and Daddy were watching
television in the front room. They heard a scratching
at the window. Daddy went to the window. Maybe
it was Anty in one of his strange moods.
"Who is it?" said Mommy.
"It's your friend, Sebastian," said Daddy.
"Oh, my God," said Mommy.

"Huh?" said God.

"Forget it," said Daddy.
"Okay," said God.
"Sebastian, depart," said Mommy.
Sebi went home to eat supper but he didn't have
much of an appetite. He ate only one can of
dog food.

There wasn't any school at the old white castle the next day. So Nora Maeve and Mommy went to Barnabas.
What's a Barnabas?
It's a basketball court with a church attached, *silly!*
The priest up on the altar was not as funny as Anty, but Nora Maeve still liked church.

But guess who came padding down the aisle right in the middle of Mass?

You're right: Sebi.

"Oh, my God!" said Mommy.

"Huh?" said God.

"Forget it," said the priest.

"Buzz off, Sebi," said Nora Maeve.

But one of the altar boys (his name was Thorstein) had to come and drag Sebi out of church.

Nora Maeve decided that she had to pray for Sebi.

"God," she said.

"Hmn..?" said God.

"I want to talk to you about Sebi."

"Ha, ha, ha, ho, ho, ho," said God.

"It's not nice to laugh at people," said Nora Maeve sternly.

"I'm sorry," said God smothering his laugh, "but if you were in my position you would do the same thing. Besides, someone has to laugh."

"Do you laugh more at little girls than at grups?" asked Nora Maeve.

"Well," said God, "grups are funnier than little children, but I've gone on record any number of times about liking little children more than anyone."

"Fine," said Nora Maeve, "then would you please make Sebi buzz off?"

God started to laugh again. "Majestic Instancy," he said.

"What?" said Nora Maeve who was now really confused.

"Forget it," said God in the midst of his laughter.

"But what about Sebi?" asked Nora Maeve.

"Leave it to me," said God. "I'll get my department of crooked lines working."

What's a crooked line?

It's the way God draws straight, *silly!*

Huh?

Forget it.

The next morning
Nora Maeve came
·out of the house.

No Sebi.

She looked behind
the garbage can.

No Sebi.

She looked under
Daddy's funny foreign car.

No Sebi.

She looked on the front steps.

She looked behind
the big old tree in the yard.

She even looked on
the swing that
she and Liam used.

Still no Sebi.

She saw Liam on his bike. Liam was the best
almost-six bike rider on the block. He wasn't tall
enough to stand on the ground when he was on
the bike. But he was still the greatest.
At least that's what he said and Daddy said so too.
So it had to be true.
"Where's Sebi, Liam?" said Nora Maeve.
Liam just shrugged his shoulders, which is pretty
hard to do when you're riding a bike.
Nora Maeve looked behind the garbage can and
under the car and in the back of the tree and on
the porch. Still no Sebi.

She went across the street to Sebi's house (which
she wasn't supposed to do) and looked in the yard.
Duncan was there munching on his breakfast,
but no Sebi.
"Duncan," said Nora Maeve, "where's Sebi?"
Duncan shrugged his shoulders—which is pretty
hard when you're a little shaggy dog.
Nora Maeve sat down right there and began to cry.
Sebi was gone.

And it was her fault.

He was really a nice dog.
He wasn't too smart and he was clumsy and kept
falling over his own feet and tripping people with
packages in their hands. But, as Mommy said, he
was only a big overgrown puppy.
He had funny ears and funny eyes and a funny
long snoot. And you couldn't ride on him like you
could on 'Nelope. And he did follow you around
every place and even come into church.
But he still was a nice dog.

Nora Maeve decided she had better go find Sebi.

So she went out on the street which didn't have a name but only a number and looked very carefully both ways as Mommy taught her to do. She crossed the street and walked down the hill to da Drive. Still no Sebi.

Now Nora Maeve knew that she really shouldn't be on da Drive. But she decided that Mommy and Daddy would certainly want her to find poor Sebi. Besides she was going to be very careful.

The teenagers came by in their cars, but Nora Maeve didn't pay any attention to them. She walked all the way down to the corner where the stop light was. Still no Sebi.

A lot of grups tried to talk to Nora Maeve. They
said silly things like, "Are you lost, little girl?"
Of course she wasn't lost. She was looking for
Sebi. But she didn't answer their questions or even
smile at them.

Nora Maeve had work to do.

She waited till the light changed to green and then, just as Mommy had told her, she looked carefully in both directions and crossed the street. "Crazy teenagers don't pay any attention to traffic signals," said Mommy.
"Look who's talking," said Anty, "about crazy teenagers."

Anyhow, Nora Maeve crossed the street and
walked by a lot of nice shops. Some had candy
in their windows and some had toys and some had
nice dresses. Nora Maeve really didn't think that
Sebi was in any of the stores, but there was no
harm in looking in the windows.

Meanwhile, back at the ranch....

Mommy was very worried. She couldn't find Nora
Maeve. She asked Liam. And all Liam knew was
that his sister had gone looking for Sebi.
Mommy called Daddy on the phone. "You'd better
come home," she said, "your daughter is lost."
But Nora Maeve wasn't lost. Sebi was lost. Nora
Maeve was looking for him. She knew where she
was. Right in front of the toy shop by the railroad
tracks.

Just then, the railroad train came by and made a terrible noise. Nora Maeve had never been that close to a train before and it scared her. To tell you the truth, it scared her very much. She decided that she'd better go home and get some help from Mommy and Daddy and Liam in finding Sebi. So she turned around to start back to da Drive.

Only da Drive wasn't there. At least Nora Maeve
couldn't find it. Which way had she come? Oh, oh.
Nora Maeve now really started to cry.
Now she and Sebi were both lost.
What's lost?
It isn't good, *silly!*

Meanwhile, back at the ranch....

Liam was worried. Mommy and Daddy were both terribly upset. They didn't blame him, but Liam figured that if you're a big boy of almost six you've got to be able to think quickly in times of emergency. Just as they do on TV. Besides, Daddy had said that Liam was part Sioux; and Indians were really good at crises.

So he went off to Barnabas (the church, not the basketball court) to discuss the matter with God.

"Hello, God," said Liam.

"Hum...Oh, Liam," said God. "Hi, what's on your mind?"

"Nora Maeve is gone," said Liam.

"What..." said God. "She can't be. My records show, let me see, yes, I thought so. Why, she's going to live to be...well, never mind that. She has a very long life expectancy and she has a lot of important things to do before we let her in up here. No, Liam, you have erroneous input. Nora Maeve is not gone."

"Then where is she?" demanded Liam, who wasn't afraid of God at all, well, not very much.

"She went to look for your friend Sebi. Oh, my God, you should excuse the expression," said God. "The crooked line department may have pushed this too far. All right, Liam, everything is under control. You go home. I'll take care of Nora Maeve."

"Okay," said Liam, "if you say so. Should I tell Mommy and Daddy that you told me it was going to be all right?"

"Hmm..." said God, "no, you'd better not. They'll think they have a mystic on their hands and there's no point in their knowing before they have to."

"Huh?" said Liam.

"Forget it," said God.

"Are you sure you can handle this," asked Liam at
the back of church.
"Don't be a heretic, young man," said God.
"What's a heretic?"
It's someone who doesn't trust God and that is
really silly, *silly!*

As soon as Liam had gone, God asked Michael who is an archangel that works for God, "Is Stanley on the crooked lines program today?" Michael didn't say why do you ask when you know it already. He thought that and God knew that he thought it so it was okay. What Michael did say was, "Yes, that's what the records show, boss."

"Stanley," said God, "what the heaven is Nora Maeve doing by the railroad tracks?"

Stanley was a new angel and still learning the trade.

"Don't worry, boss," he said kind of nervously, "I kept the train from hitting her."

"Fine, Stanley," said God gently, "but she didn't have to be scared that much to know not to disobey Mommy. Get her headed back toward da Drive."

"That's a rookie," said Michael.

"You said it," said God with a sigh.

I bet none of you knew that there are rookie angels.

"Sebi," said God.
"Huh?" said Sebi.
"Wake up, you lazy Labrador," said God, "I've got work for you."
"Yes, boss," said Sebi and immediately started running down the street in the wrong direction.

Fortunately, he fell over his big feet.

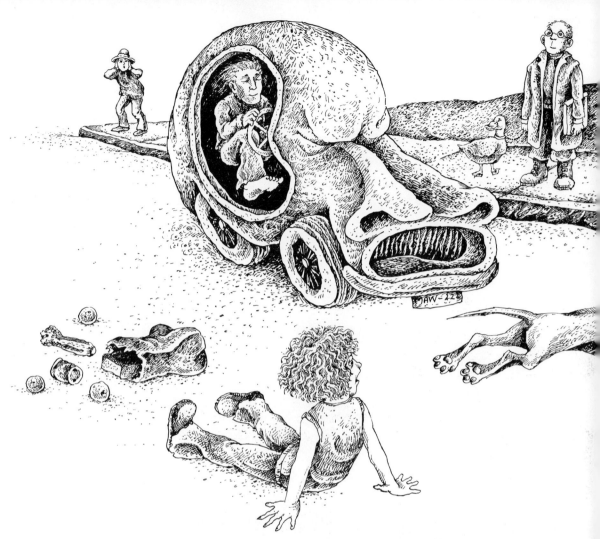

God sighed again. He had made Labradors the way
they are but sometimes they can be a trial. "Sebi,"
said God, "hotfoot it over to the railroad tracks and
retrieve Nora Maeve."
Sebi headed for the tracks about twice as fast as
Liam did when he drove his bike at top speed.
Poor Stanley had to keep a teenager in a Ferrari
from running Sebi over.
"And when you find her, bring her to the castle
until Daddy gets there," God shouted after him.

Sebi ran so fast that he ran right by Nora Maeve
and on toward the railroad tracks. Michael had to
whistle at him to turn around.
"Sebi," shouted Nora Maeve, "I've found you!"
Sebi turned around and came back—again at full
speed. He skidded to a stop where Nora Maeve
was.
She stopped crying and hugged Sebi. "I wasn't
lost at all," she said.

"Just like Daniel Boone," said God,
"only a little bewildered."

Sebi jumped up and down,

he rolled over,

he ran in circles,

he barked.

He was so happy he thought he would explode.

"I thought you were a retriever," said Stanley.
Sebi became very serious. It was now time to be
a professional retriever. He began to sniff the
ground to find the trail back to the castle. Nora
Maeve took his collar and the two of them very
slowly and carefully went by all the stores (and
they didn't look in the windows once) back toward
the castle on da Drive.

Meanwhile, back at the ranch....

Daddy and Liam were in Daddy's funny foreign car looking for Nora Maeve. They looked at grandma's house. They looked at nana's house. They looked at the house where the other Nora and 'Nelope and Muffie lived. No Nora Maeve.

They looked at the park and at Barnabas (both the court and the church) and at Sutherland (where the publics go to school); still no Nora Maeve.

They went up and down all the streets in the neighborhood and talked to all the boys and girls they saw. Not a trace of Nora Maeve.

"Liam," said God.
"Huh?" said Liam.
"Tell Daddy to go look at the white castle where Nora Maeve goes to school."
"Check, boss," said Liam.
Daddy turned the car onto da Drive, narrowly missing a hit from a crazy teenager.
"I bet I know where she is," said Liam.
"Where?" asked Daddy.
"I bet she's at the old white castle," said Liam.
"Why would she be there?" said Daddy.
"You know how she likes school," said Liam; "girls are that way."
"Check," said Daddy.

And sure enough, when Daddy and Liam and the
funny foreign car came up to the old white castle
there was Nora Maeve and Sebi, sitting on the
steps. Sebi was wagging his tail. When Nora
Maeve saw the car she thought maybe she should
cry, just in case Daddy would be mad.
Daddy was a little angry at first, but he was so
glad to have Nora Maeve back that he got over it
real quick. Daddies are that way with little girls.
Nora Maeve laughed. "Sebi was lost and I had to
find him."

When they got home, Mommy said very sternly, "Nora Maeve, don't you ever do that again." But she was glad to have her back too.

"At least she didn't cross the drive," said Mommy. Nora Maeve didn't say anything at all.

"Look, Nora Maeve," said God, "Mommy and Daddy and Liam don't know you crossed da Drive, but I do, and so does Sebi and Stanley and Michael. Don't ever do it again. You can't expect God to get you out of trouble every time you disobey Mommy."

"Check, boss," said Nora Maeve.

She thought for a minute and then said, "God?"

"Huh?" said God.

"I think Mommy knows I crossed da Drive. Mommies know everything."

"I know what you mean," said God, "but don't do it again anyway."

"No way, forget it," said Nora Maeve.

That night when she was going to bed Nora Maeve said her prayers. She was thankful that Sebi was not lost anymore and she was sorry Mommy and Daddy and Liam had worried about her. She said she loved Mommy and Daddy and Sebi and Liam and the other Nora and Duncan and Katie and Anty and God.

"Lots of surrogates down there, Mickey," said God
to Michael. "You notice we got final billing."
"That's the way you built the place, boss," said
Michael, "just as you told that Job fellow when
he got pushy."
"Check," said God.

Sebi got a big bone and a huge pitcher of warm milk and no one ever chased him away from Nora Maeve's house ever again.
You wouldn't believe how happy he is, unless maybe you have a Labrador.

That night after Liam and Nora Maeve had gone to bed and were sound asleep, Anty came by. Mommy and Daddy told him the story of Sebi being "lost" and Nora Maeve "finding" him. They didn't know about God and Michael and Stanley, of course.
"That's a great story," said Anty, "down the nights and down the years."
"Now you will go write a book about it," Daddy said.
"No way, forget it," said Anty.

"Want to bet?" said God.

And they all lived happily ever after—well,
more or less.